To those who give without looking back
and those who receive without forgetting
—D.R.

Text copyright © 2011 by David Rubel
Jacket art and interior illustrations copyright © 2011 by Jim LaMarche
Photograph credits: Jacket photograph and p. 45: copyright © Habitat for Humanity International/Steffan Hacker;
p. 44: © 2011 Rockefeller Group Inc./Rockefeller Center Archives

Visit us on the Web! www.randomhouse.com/kids

Educators and librarians, for a variety of teaching tools, visit us at www.randomhouse.com/teachers

Library of Congress Cataloging-in-Publication Data
Rubel, David.
The carpenter's gift / by David Rubel ; illustrated by Jim LaMarche. — 1st ed.
p. cm.
Summary: In Depression-era New York City, construction workers at the Rockefeller Center site help a family in need—a gift that is repaid years later in the donation of an enormous Christmas tree.
ISBN 978-0-375-86922-8 (trade) — ISBN 978-0-375-96922-5 (lib. bdg.) — ISBN 978-0-375-98933-9 (ebook)
[1. Kindness—Fiction. 2. Christmas trees—Fiction. 3. Rockefeller Center—Fiction.] I. LaMarche, Jim, ill. II. Title.
PZ7.R8279Car 2011 [E]—dc22 2010033203

MANUFACTURED IN MALAYSIA

10 9 8 7 6 5 4 3 2 1

First Edition

The Carpenter's Gift

A Christmas Tale About the Rockefeller Center Tree

BY DAVID RUBEL • ILLUSTRATED BY JIM LaMARCHE

RANDOM HOUSE NEW YORK

*N*early a lifetime had passed, but Henry could still remember what it felt like to wake up in the old shack, especially during wintertime. In those days, the Great Depression gripped the country, and like many people, Henry's parents were out of work. They couldn't afford coal for the stove or warm blankets for the beds, so young Henry usually woke up with a shiver. But he didn't complain, because it was nobody's fault. Instead, he visited warm places in his mind.

One day in 1931—actually, the day before Christmas—Henry was reading a book when he heard the loud *toot-toot* of a car horn. He opened the front door and saw his father behind the wheel of a borrowed truck.

"Go for a ride, Sparky?" his father shouted over the rumbling engine.

"You bet!" Henry shouted back, and raced inside to get his coat. Riding in any sort of car was a special treat for Henry, not to be missed. Soon, he was sitting beside his father—nose pressed to the window glass.

They drove into a nearby grove of evergreens. Henry breathed in the strong, familiar smell.

"Here's the plan," Henry's father said. "See those spruce trees, Sparky? We're going to cut them down and take them to the city."

"Why?" Henry asked.

"To sell them as Christmas trees!" his father said.

Even though New York City was just an hour's drive away, Henry had never been there before. He shivered with excitement at the thought of seeing all those tall buildings scraping the sky.

When Henry and his father reached Midtown Manhattan, they began looking for
a place to park and unload. Driving down Fifth Avenue, they found a good spot next
to a construction site.

"Mind if I set up here?" Henry's father asked a worker.

The man looked them over. It didn't take him long to figure out that Henry's father
was down on his luck.

"No problem," the man said. "I'll give you a hand. My name's Frank." Then he
turned around and called out, "Hey, Mikey, Paulie! Help me out here!"

For the rest of the afternoon, Henry and his father sold trees to passersby.
By the end of the day, they had earned enough money to make the trip a success.

"We should be getting home now," Henry's father said as the sun set behind
a tall building.

"What about the rest of the trees?" Henry asked.

"I thought we'd give them to Frank and the other fellows."

Henry nodded in agreement. *The best presents are the ones you don't expect,*
he thought.

Because it was Christmas Eve, the workers were having a little party. Frank and the others took the tallest of the trees that Henry and his father had given them and decorated it with whatever they could cobble together: paper garlands, cranberries threaded onto string, and even a few shiny tin cans. Henry added an ornament of his own, made of newspaper that he folded into a star.

In the background, he could hear his father talking with Frank about grown-up things: the hard times for Henry's family, the shack in which they lived. But Henry didn't want to think about those things. He just wanted to look at the most marvelous Christmas tree he had ever seen.

It had been the best day that Henry could remember, and he didn't want it to end. He stood before the decorated tree, enchanted. The streetlamps had just come on, and the tin cans glittered in their light. *If ever there was a magic moment,* Henry thought, *this is it.*

He decided to make a special Christmas wish. He wished that one day his family would live in a nice, warm house.

After making his wish, Henry opened his eyes. His gaze fell on a pinecone lying on the ground. He picked it up and was turning it over in his hands when he felt his father's grip on his shoulder.

"Time to go, Sparky," his father said.

Henry stuffed the pinecone in his pocket, said good night to the workers, and walked with his father back to the truck.

By the time they arrived home, it was well past Henry's bedtime.

"You must be exhausted," his mother said, slipping off his boots.

"Straight to bed with you."

Shrugging off his coat, Henry felt a bulge in his pocket. It was the
pinecone. He took it out and looked at it, remembering the joys of
the day and the magic of the tree.

The next morning, Henry's parents let him sleep late. In fact, it was well past eight when the *toot-toot* of several car horns woke him.

Rushing to the window, he saw three trucks pulling up outside. All were loaded with lumber and other building supplies. At the wheel of the first truck was Frank, and behind him were other Rockefeller Center workers. What were they doing so far from the city on Christmas morning?

Frank got out of the truck. "After you left, we got to thinking," he said. "There was all this extra wood lying around, and we had the day off, so we thought we'd drive up and see what we could do to help you with this house of yours."

Frank looked the shack over, taking in its patched walls and ill-fitting windows.

"I think we'll have to make a fresh start," he said.

Henry's father didn't have words for the way he felt, so he simply took Frank's hand and shook it.

The sound of sawing and hammering traveled far enough that Christmas morning for Henry's neighbors to wonder what was going on. A few walked over, saw the new house going up, and spread the word. By midafternoon, a dozen more people were pitching in.

As the new house took shape, Frank called Henry over. "See those boards?" he said, pointing to a stack of cedar. "We're going to use them to trim the windows, but they've got nails in them. I need you to pull the nails out."

Henry moved to fetch the boards, but Frank called him back. Digging into his toolbox, he handed Henry an old claw hammer. "You'll be needing this," Frank said.

By nightfall, the frame of the new house was nearly done. By week's end, it had a roof. Soon enough, it was ready for Henry and his family to move in.

In the spring, Henry's parents celebrated with a potluck dinner. They invited everyone who had helped build the house. Henry was glad to see Frank again. He was ready to return the claw hammer, but Frank wouldn't take it. "You keep it, son," he said. "It may come in handy someday."

After dinner, Henry sat happily in his very own room. He thought about his Christmas wish and couldn't believe it had actually come true! He knew he should do something special to express how thankful he was, and he thought long and hard about what that might be. Finally, he decided to plant the pinecone. Maybe he could be Jack from the beanstalk story, and the pinecone could be his magic bean.

Henry planted the pinecone beside the new house. In time, a seedling emerged. Henry watered and weeded it. As time passed, both he and the tree grew tall and strong. Henry especially liked to hammer away in its shade, and he became quite a good carpenter, building many projects with his skilled hands.

As Henry grew up, however, he became busy with other things. He got married, moved away, and had a family. Most summers, though, he returned to visit his parents. On lazy days, he sat beneath the tree with his son, teaching him how to build things with the old claw hammer.

As he got even older, Henry sometimes wondered where the time went. One day, he was a young boy, waking up with a shiver. The next, he was an old man, living alone. Not needing a big place anymore, he decided to move back into the house where he had grown up.

To keep himself busy, Henry began working on the house, which was showing its age. He especially liked using the old claw hammer. Its polished handle, smooth and dark from wear, felt comfortable in his hand.

One day, as Henry worked on the front porch, a man drove up to see him. The man told Henry that he worked for Rockefeller Center and that it was his job to pick out the new Christmas tree each year.

"I just love your spruce!" the man said. "When I saw it from my helicopter yesterday, I knew that it had to be this year's tree."

Henry wasn't sure what to do. He knew that being asked was an honor. But he and the tree had been together a long time, and he was reluctant to let it go.

"I know that I'm asking a lot," the man said. "But if you agree, I can promise you that your tree will bring joy to millions of people."

Henry thought some more.

"And when the holiday season is over," the man continued, "we mill the tree and use the lumber to help a family in need build a new home."

A family in need? Suddenly, Henry felt a shiver, and the calendar in his mind
flipped back to 1931—driving to New York City with his father, meeting Frank and
the other workers, building the house, planting the tree. He knew what he had to do.

"I've been given so much," Henry said. "I want to give something back. The tree
is yours."

Just before Thanksgiving, Henry received an invitation to the tree lighting. On the special day, a car picked him up and drove him all the way to Rockefeller Center, where he met the family whose new home would be built with the tree's lumber. They hugged him and thanked him many times for his generosity.

Afterward, Henry stood off to the side and watched the family's young daughter. "It's so beautiful," the girl said softly as she stared up at the enormous tree.

Then something caught the child's eye. A pinecone had fallen to the ground. Picking it up, she turned it over and over in her hands before stuffing it into her pocket.

If ever there was a magic moment, Henry thought, *this is it.*

Henry walked over to the girl, and they stood together, gazing at the glittering tree. Then Henry reached into his coat pocket and pulled out the old claw hammer. "Here you go, Sparky," Henry said. "You'll be needing this."

The first Rockefeller Center Christmas tree in December 1931

ABOUT THE CHRISTMAS TREE AT ROCKEFELLER CENTER

Since 1933, countless New Yorkers—and countless visitors to the city—have come to Rockefeller Center to marvel at the world's most famous Christmas tree. Adults who visited the tree as youngsters now bring their children and grandchildren to share in the amazement.

The first tree was erected by construction workers digging the foundation for Rockefeller Center in 1931. They wanted to show their appreciation for having jobs at a time—the Great Depression—when so many others were out of work. The twenty-foot tree, which they pooled their money to buy, was decorated with garlands and other ornaments handmade by their families.

Today, the Christmas trees that grace Rockefeller Center are much grander, measuring seventy to one hundred feet tall and about forty feet wide. Each is decorated with thirty thousand multicolored LED lights strung on five miles of wire.

Tree selection begins with helicopter flights over New York, New Jersey, and New England. Using a laptop computer equipped with GPS, the chief gardener of Rockefeller Center records the locations of promising trees and then visits them on the ground.

Once the choice is made, a team of twenty arborists fells the tree and uses a 280-ton all-terrain crane to lower it onto a custom-built trailer. When the trailer and its police escort reach Midtown Manhattan, the crane lifts the tree onto a platform beside the Rockefeller Center skating rink.

The annual tree lighting is a spectacular event, attended by crowds of New Yorkers and tourists and watched on television by people around the world. It takes place the week following Thanksgiving. In 2007, a new tradition began when Tishman Speyer, the company that owns Rockefeller Center, began donating the wood from the tree to Habitat for Humanity. Habitat uses this lumber to help families in need build affordable homes.

To learn more about the Christmas tree and the history of Rockefeller Center, visit rockefellercenter.com.

About Habitat for Humanity International

Nearly two billion people around the world lack adequate shelter. The mission of Habitat for Humanity International is to help as many of these people as possible build simple, decent homes in which to live safely, healthfully, and affordably.

Habitat's two thousand affiliates work locally to organize building projects. Donations finance the supplies, and volunteers provide most of the labor. Even so, the homes are not free. The partner families contribute hundreds of hours of labor and also pay for the homes through nonprofit mortgages. Their monthly payments fund more Habitat homes.

"You can see the pride in the faces of the partner families on the day that they receive the keys to their new home," Habitat's most famous volunteer, former president Jimmy Carter, has observed. "They know that they aren't being given a handout but a hand up, because they have done their share of the work and they will be paying their share of the cost."

Just as building Habitat homes remakes the lives of these families, so does it transform the lives of volunteers. Many had long wanted to help people in need but didn't know how until Habitat gave them an opportunity. Now they return to build again and again because of the way that helping makes them feel. Most have found that no matter how hard they work, they always get more in return than they put in.

Habitat, an ecumenical Christian ministry, welcomes all people to volunteer. Since its founding in 1976, it has built more than 400,000 homes around the world—providing simple, decent, affordable housing for two million people.

To learn more about the work of Habitat for Humanity International, visit habitat.org.

Pilson Kipkirui of Kenya outside the simple home his family built with Habitat